Rita and the
Romans

Rita and the Romans

Hilda Offen

Happy Cat Books

For Jodie and Laura

HAPPY CAT BOOKS

Published by Happy Cat Books Ltd.
Bradfield, Essex CO11 2UT, UK

First published 2002
3 5 7 9 10 8 6 4 2

Copyright © Hilda Offen, 2002
The moral right of the author/illustrator has been asserted
All rights reserved

A CIP catalogue record for this book is available from the British Library

ISBN 1 903285 40 2

Printed in China by Midas Printing Limited

"It's Roman Day at the Sports Field!" said
Julie. "I'm going to the mosaic class."
"I'm a trumpeter," said Jim.
"And I'm the Standard Bearer for the
Roman army!" said Eddie. "We've
got a giant catapult. We're going
to fight the Picts."

"Can I come?" asked Rita.

"No!" said Eddie. "You haven't got a costume."

"I have! I have!" cried Rita. "I've got a toga in my dressing-up box. Please wait for me!"

"Not likely !" said Eddie.

They pulled the garden roller across the Wendy-house door and ran off to the Sports Field.

Rita pushed and pushed but the door wouldn't budge.
"Huh!" she thought. "It's a good thing I've got my Rescuer outfit in here."

Rita was so furious that she changed in double-quick time. Then she dived at the floor, whirring round and round like a drill. She burst out through a flower-bed and headed for the Sports Field.

The mosaic class was in uproar.
"It's those jackdaws from the castle ruins!" said the teacher. "They keep stealing the blue bits!"
"Leave it to me," said Rita.
She flew to the top of the castle.
"You should be ashamed of yourselves!" she said to the jackdaws.

"Sorry!" they squawked.
"Blue's our favourite colour."
"And what's this shiny bird?" asked Rita.
"We found it!" said the jackdaws. "Honest!"

Rita tucked the bird in her belt and flew
back with the mosaic pieces.
"Oh, thank you, Rescuer!" cried the teacher.
"Now we can get on."
"And so can I!" said Rita. She could hear
someone nearby, puffing and blowing like a
walrus.
It was Adrian Oakley, the builder.

"What's up?" asked Rita.

"I've promised to build this wall in time for the battle," puffed Mr. Oakley. "But the blocks are too heavy. I'm not going to get it done."

"Cheer up, Mr Oakley!" said Rita. "I'll help you."

"Oh, thanks, Rescuer!" said Mr Oakley. "And please - call me Adrian."

"Right-ho, Adrian!" said Rita. "Let's get to work on this wall."

They were finished in no time.

Adrian's Wall

"That should keep the Picts out," said Rita.
"Uh-oh! Time to go!"
Someone was roaring "YOU'VE DONE
WHAT?"
A Roman Centurion was glaring at Eddie.
"What do you mean, you've 'lost the
eagle'?" he roared.
"It must have dropped off," said Eddie.
"We can't go into battle without our eagle!"
shouted the Centurion.

"Is this what you're looking for?" asked
Rita. "I found it in a jackdaw's nest."
"Phew!" said Eddie. "Thanks, Rescuer."

"Romans! Forward march!"
roared the Centurion. "Man
the catapult!"
The Picts were really the
local cricket team. They
peeped over the wall and
stuck out their tongues.

No-one noticed a
toddler climbing into
the catapult.

"Load the ammunition!" cried the
Centurion. "Fire!"
The crowd gasped.

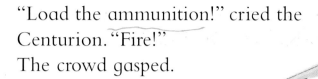

"Oh dear!" said the Centurion as the toddler
whizzed overhead. "Oh dear!"

But Rita had seen what was happening. She
shot through the air and caught the toddler
in the nick of time.
"Well held!" cried the Picts.
"Oh, thank you, Rescuer!" cried the toddler's
mother. "He's into everything these days."

All at once the crowd caught its breath.
A little girl had wandered on to the track!
"She'll be trampled!" they cried.
But Rita had seen the danger.

She swooped down and snatched the little
girl from under the ponies' hooves.

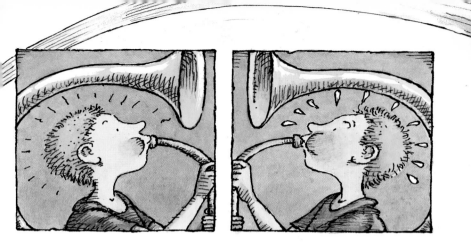

"Settle down, everyone!" cried the announcer when the battle was over. "Time for the Chariot Race!"

It was Jim's big moment. He raised his trumpet and blew. Nothing happened. He blew and he blew but not a sound came out.

"Let's see what I can do!" said Rita.

She gave an enormous puff – and out shot a potato! TAA-RAA! went the trumpet – and the race was on!

Round and round the course thundered the chariots, pulled by the two fittest ponies in the pony club.

"Hello, Rescuer!" said the little girl. "Would you like a daisy?"

"Oh – thanks!" said Rita. Below them the ponies thundered over the finishing line and everyone cheered.

"Now - the moment you've been waiting for!" cried the announcer. "Here come the Gladiators!"
A lion and a gladiator ran into the arena and saluted each other. Then the fight began.

They were interrupted by a savage howl as
Basher Briggs and his dog burst from the crowd.
"Go on, Monster, grab'em!" yelled Basher.
"I'm off!" whimpered the gladiator.
"Rip!" The lion costume tore apart.
The front legs went one way and
the back legs the other.

Rita ran into the arena and whispered in
Monster's ear. He stopped barking and rolled
on his back while Rita tickled his tummy.
Then he ran off into the crowd.

"Basher! You need a lesson!" said Rita. She speared Basher's cap with the trident and threw the net over him.

"Hooray!" yelled the crowd.
"Hooray for the Rescuer!"
"Shall I let him go or hook him
on the flagpole?" Rita asked.
The crowd gave the
thumbs-down sign.
"Hook him on the flagpole!"
they roared. So Rita did.

Then Rita entered some competitions. She guessed the number of pickled walnuts, she won the javelin contest and she defeated the champion wrestler.

...and be kind to your little sisters!

Have your say!

After that she entered the Public Speaking
Competition. She told some good jokes and
made everyone laugh; and she said a few
thoughtful things, too.

"Well done, Rescuer!" said the mayor.
"You're the winner!"
"Oh, thank you!" said Rita. "I'm honoured!"
And she flew away over the Sports Field and
back to the Wendy-house.

It wasn't long before Eddie, Julie and Jim
came rushing down the path. They pulled
away the roller.

"Sorry, Rita!" said Jim. "You've missed the
Rescuer again – she was amazing."

"We've got you some honeycakes," said
Julie. "And a snake bracelet – it's meant to
bring you luck."

"Thank you!" said Rita. "If it works, I might
even get to see the Rescuer one day."